PATRICK PICKLEBOTTOM
EVERYDAY MYSTERIES

The CASE of the
BRAZILIAN
VASE

BOOK ONE

MR. JAY

NEW PAIGE PRESS

An imprint of Lyric & Stone Publishing, LLC

New Paige Press, LLC
NewPaigePress.com

New Paige Press and colophon are registered trademarks
of New Paige Press, LLC.

Text copyright © 2023 by New Paige Press
Illustrations copyright © 2023 by Gary Wilkinson
Interior design by Melinda Martin

ISBN 978-1-958514-07-8

Printed and bound in China

New Paige Press provides special discounts when purchased in
larger volumes for premiums and promotional purposes, as well
as for fundraising and educational use. Custom editions can
also be created for special purposes. In addition, supplemental
teaching material can be provided upon request. For more
information, please visit LyricandStone.com.

New Paige Press is an imprint of Lyric & Stone Publishing, LLC

How to read
"Patrick Picklebottom's Everyday Mysteries!"

Hello, and thank you for reading this book! Ever since I first created this character in my picture book, *Patrick Picklebottom and the Penny Book,* I've wanted to do more with him and create new adventures for Patrick and his friends.

The idea for *Everyday Mysteries* came to me when I began to think about some of the books that I loved to read when I was growing up. As a young boy, some of my favorite books were in the *Encyclopedia Brown* collection, written by Donald J. Sobol. It was always so much fun to read each adventure and try to solve the mysteries myself — I would read each one over and over again, even after I already knew the solution!

So I began to think that I could do something similar with Patrick Picklebottom. As a boy who loves books and has an expanded imagination along with a love of critical thinking, Patrick feels like the perfect character to take on everyday mysteries.

There are 10 completely different stories in this book, that can be read in any order. And because they can be read in any order, you'll notice a little bit of repetition from one story to the next — for example, I mention who key characters are, like Claire and Roger, over and over again, because I don't know which story you'll start with, and if you don't know who the characters are, the story might not make a lot of sense to you. But I try to do this as little as possible to keep each story fun to read.

More importantly, each story is a small mystery that *you* get to solve. For most stories, the mystery can be solved simply by using the clues that are in the story. Think about them carefully before jumping to the end of the book and reading the solution — I bet if you read the story again, and really think about it, you'll be able to solve it!

There are a few stories, though, that you may need to do some extra research for. If I think a mystery needs a little more research to solve, I'll say so at the end. For these stories, ask your parents or teacher to help you use the Internet and search for topics in the story that may help you find the solution.

I hope you enjoy reading this book as much as I enjoyed writing it. Now . . . go solve some mysteries, detective!

— MR. JAY

Table of Contents

The Brazilian Artifact

I t was just before noon, and Patrick Picklebottom was sitting on the floor of his room, reading the new book he had bought the day before. Downstairs, he could hear his little sister playing video games and angrily yelling at the TV screen. From outside his window wafted the smell of freshly cut grass. His father had been mowing the lawn since finishing breakfast an hour earlier — his typical Saturday morning routine.

Patrick was fully engrossed in his book, and had just reached the most exciting chapter, when he was jolted back to reality by his best friend, Claire, who was standing at his bedroom door. "Earth to Patrick! Hey, can you hear me?"

"Huh?" Patrick asked, looking confused. "Sorry, Claire, I didn't see you. What did you say?"

"No kidding you didn't see me — I've been standing here trying to get your attention for, like, an hour!" Claire had a flair for exaggeration. Patrick guessed she had actually only been standing there for about thirty seconds, but he didn't push her on it.

"Sorry," he repeated, "I was just really into this book."

"What else is new? You're always into a book," Claire said sarcastically. "Meanwhile, you're missing a beautiful day outside! Come on, let's go do something!" And without waiting for his reply, Claire turned and bounded down the hallway, gave a quick "See you later, Mrs. P!" to his mom, and headed outside, where she'd left her bike.

Patrick sighed and reluctantly put down his book. He knew there was no arguing with Claire when she was in this mood. Besides, he figured, he could always finish his book later, before bed.

After getting his bike out of the garage, he met Claire at the base of his driveway. "Okay, so where do you want to go?" he asked, pushing his hair back and putting on his helmet.

"I don't know. I saw some signs for yard sales a few blocks over. Want to go check them out?"

"Sure! Yard sales almost always have boxes of great old books for sale, for practically nothing!" Patrick said, finally feeling excited.

Claire rolled her eyes. "You and your books!" Once she had strapped on her helmet, the pair took off down Maple Avenue. They turned left onto Sullivan Way, cut through the school yard, and came to a particularly large yard sale at a small yellow house with bright blue trim.

Patrick knew the house well, but had never been inside; Roger Wigglesworth lived there. Roger was a particularly nasty kid in his grade, who was always bragging about expensive games he had, or impressive things he had done. Roger especially liked to talk about his many athletic talents, although Patrick couldn't recall him doing anything all that that extraordinary in gym class.

Before Patrick could protest, Claire was already off her bike and making her way through the small crowd of customers and around to each of the piles of items for sale, looking for hidden treasures. Patrick followed her, half-heartedly keeping an eye out for any books that looked interesting, but was

"...I dug it up myself!" Roger said,
showing off what seemed to be a very old vase.

determined not to buy anything that Roger Wigglesworth was selling.

After a few minutes of looking around, Patrick was about ready to tell Claire he wanted to explore another yard sale a few houses over, when he heard Roger's voice just off to his left.

"...I dug it up myself!" Roger said, showing off what seemed to be a very old vase. It was brownish, with faded blue specks peeking out from behind a thin layer of caked-on dirt, and an intricate spiral design along the edging at the top. One of the handles was still intact, while the other had been broken off around the middle.

Patrick's friend, Tommy, a known history buff, was looking at the vase with interest, as Roger continued, "I went on a dig in Brazil last summer as part of an elite 'Young Archeologists' program. I was the only one selected out of over a thousand entries, partially because I speak Spanish, so I could talk to the natives there, but mostly because they said that I wrote the best essay about the importance of preserving ancient artifacts that they had ever read in over twenty years.

"Anyway, we had been digging in this remote area just outside a rain forest for weeks. Everyone was on the verge of giving up, when suddenly I hit something solid with my hand shovel. At first, I thought it was just another rock, but when I cleared the dirt away, I saw that it wasn't a rock at all — it was this vase! Of course, it was much dirtier then than it is now. I was able to clean it off a little, but some of this dirt is here to stay, I think. That didn't matter though. What mattered was that I had found an artifact that proved that an ancient civilization had been there! They continued to dig, and eventually we found a whole village, and it would never have been discovered if it weren't for me. The whole team was so excited about it that they let me keep this vase as a souvenir! It's the best thing I own!"

Tommy's eyes were wide with wonder, as a small "Wow!" escaped his lips. "How much are you selling it for?" he asked anxiously.

"Oooh, I don't know," Roger said, looking incredulous. "This is my prized possession. I don't know if I'd be able to part with it. This is an important, valuable historical artifact. I mean . . . I don't think I'd be able to sell it for less than $50, and even that would be a steal."

Tommy pursed his lips and opened his wallet, looking at its contents. "That's all the money I have, and it took me over a year to save it. But wow, this is such a great vase, and right from an authentic archeological dig! It's worth it — I'll give you $50 for it!"

But just as Tommy was about to hand over his life's savings, Patrick reached out and grabbed his arm. "Wait a minute, Tommy. Save your money — I don't know if that vase has any historical value, but I know that Roger's story isn't worth a penny. He made it all up!"

How did Patrick know that Roger was lying?

Hint: You may need to do some extra research to solve this one.

What do you think you should look up?

Turn to page 84 for the answer.

The Stolen Bicycle

"**S**o what flavor are you getting?" Patrick Picklebottom asked, wiping his forehead with his already sweat-drenched t-shirt.

"At this point, I don't really care," his friend Claire said, fanning herself a little dramatically. "What is it? Like 500 degrees outside today? I'll take any flavor that will cool me down. But probably chocolate. With peanut butter chips. And maybe some rainbow sprinkles."

"I'm not sure it's 500 degrees out," Patrick said as they reached the entrance to the ice cream parlor. Looking at the digital sign at the bank across the street, he saw that it was 1:04 p.m., and 97 degrees out. "But it is *really* hot. It's even worse than it was yesterday, and yesterday was brutal. My feet are squishing in my sneakers from the sweat!"

"Gross, Patrick. I didn't need to know that."

Patrick chuckled as they entered the ice cream

shop. Inside, a number of other kids were already waiting in line or happily enjoying their ice cream cones. Only one kid didn't look happy to be there. In the back corner, Alastair Bingstipple was sitting by himself, wearing a dusty baseball uniform, and staring angrily at an untouched strawberry milkshake on the table in front of him.

Patrick and Claire made their way over. "Hey, Alastair!" Patrick said jovially. "Great game today! You hit the longest home run I've ever seen!"

An hour earlier, Patrick and Claire had left Snuffleberry Park after watching a little league baseball game between the Pythons and the Atomic Gnats. Even though Alastair was a year younger and a full grade lower than most of his teammates, he was the Atomic Gnats' star player — a talented shortstop and a powerful hitter. The game has been tied 3 to 3, when Alastair hit a solo homer in the ninth inning to score the game-winning run.

"Thanks," Alastair said miserably.

Patrick and Claire looked at each other quizzically. "So why the long face there, superstar?" Claire asked. "You look like someone just stole your dog."

Alastair looked at her. "Close. My dog is home, safe and sound. It was my bike that got stolen."

"What do you mean?" Patrick asked, taking a seat at the table.

Claire sat down as well. "Whoa, that's terrible!" she said. "I totally want to hear all about this . . . but, you know, if you're not gonna drink that milkshake . . ."

Alastair took a deep breath and pushed the untouched milkshake over to Claire, who tried (unsuccessfully) to hide her smile as she took a big sip of it. He sat back in his chair, took his base-ball cap off, and ran his hand through his hair in frustration. "After the game was finished, I hung around to celebrate with my team. We were there for half an hour or so, and then I went to go get my bike from behind the third base dugout where I left it, and it was gone."

"Did you have it chained up to anything?" Patrick asked.

Alastair shook his head, "No. I mean, maybe I should have, but there were a million people there watching the game. I guess I didn't think about it. Who would to steal a bike with all those other people around?"

Claire wiped some strawberry milkshake from her chin. "I get that. I would do the same thing. We don't get a lot of bike thefts in this town," she pointed out, in between gulps.

Patrick glanced at her, and rolled his eyes. Turning back to Alastair, he asked, "Everyone else seemed to leave the game around the same time we did, right after you hit that home run. Did you notice anyone besides your teammates still hanging around?"

"Yeah, Roger Wigglesworth was still there, watching us celebrate for a while. He seemed annoyed, which makes sense since his younger brother is on the Pythons."

Roger Wigglesworth was a particularly obnoxious kid in Patrick and Claire's grade. His brother, Mort, was in Alister's grade, and was the pitcher for the Pythons.

"Yeah, neither of them really like to lose," Patrick considered.

"Who does?" asked Claire, wiping the last few drops of strawberry milkshake from her chin.

"Claire . . . ugh, never mind." Patrick waived her off and turned back to Alastair. "So do you think Roger stole your bike?"

Alister shrugged. "Maybe. I don't really know him that well. I mean, I know he can be a jerk, but I wouldn't have guessed he's a thief, too."

"Well," Patrick said, standing up, "there's only one way to find out! Let's go to Roger's house and ask him. He doesn't live far from here."

The three got up and left the ice cream shop, walking right back out into the sweltering heat. They walked down the street, past the library and to the other side of the park where the baseball game had just been played. Two blocks past the park, they reached the small yellow house with blue shutters where Roger lived.

Claire was acting as though they had crossed the desert. "I think . . . I think I need another ice cream," she said, exasperated.

"I think you'll be fine," Patrick said, although he did have to admit that the heat was getting worse, as he wiped the sweat from his forehead.

Outside the house, Roger was sitting in a rocking chair on the front porch, fanning himself with a book in one hand and holding a drink with the other. He rocked back and forth slowly, eyeing the three, but not making any effort to get up or greet them.

"Well," said Patrick, looking around the yard, "I don't see your bike anywhere, but that doesn't mean it's not here. As much as I usually try to avoid it, let's go talk to Roger."

Roger sat and watched the three cross his yard and approach the front porch. Although he didn't say anything, a small look of amusement seemed to cross his face.

"Hi Roger," Patrick said flatly.

Roger glared at him, stirring his tall glass of Fizzy's Lemonade with a straw, the ice clinking against the glass. He looked at each of them in turn. "Okay, so, hi. What do you guys want?"

Claire was eyeing his drink thirstily, like a dog staring up at a delicious treat. "Hi, Roger," she said, sounding as friendly as she possibly could.

"Any chance I can I get a glass of Fizzy's Lemonade, too? It's so hot out!"

Roger continued to rock in his chair, the smirk on his face getting a little larger. "Sorry, but I locked myself out of the house, and can't get back in until my parents come home with the keys. Here, though," Roger said as he put two of his sweaty fingers inside of his drink and pulled out an ice cube. "You can have this to cool yourself off."

He tossed the ice cube to Claire, who jumped back in disgust. "Ew, no thanks. That's gross."

Roger chortled. "Okay, have it your way. But I know you guys didn't come to share a lemonade with me. So why are you really here?"

Alastair, who had been brooding in the background, suddenly spoke up. "You stole my bike, and I want it back!" he shouted. The smirk on Roger's face quickly disappeared, and he leaned forward in his chair, menacingly. "Are you calling me a thief?"

Patrick quickly stepped between them. "Nobody's calling you anything. Alastair's bike was stolen after

Roger tossed the ice cube to Claire, who jumped back in disgust.

"Ew, no thanks. That's just gross."

the baseball game today, and he saw you hanging around the park after the game was over. We wanted to see if you knew anything about it."

Roger sat back in his chair and took a long sip from his drink. "You must have me confused with somebody else. I left after the seventh inning. Came home, got myself this nice, cool glass of lemonade." He took another long sip and smirked at Claire, who was fanning herself furiously from the heat. "I came out onto the porch, and I've been here ever since, reading this book and not stealing bicycles."

Patrick tried to push a bit more, but hesitated to accuse Roger of anything just yet. "Then you wouldn't mind if we looked inside the house, just to be sure?"

Roger didn't miss a beat. "Ordinarily I'd love to ask you inside. But like I said, I locked myself out of the house after I came home. I'd invite you wait around until my parents get back later, but since I don't like any of you, why don't you just make like a drum and beat it, instead?"

Patrick chewed his lip for a second, then looked

at Roger and said, "Not just yet. I can't prove that you stole the bike, but I do know you made up this whole story, and you wouldn't do that if you didn't have something to hide. So why don't you just give Alastair his bike back, so we can get out of here?"

How did Patrick know Roger was lying?

Hint: No additional research is needed — all of the clues you need for this one are right in the story!

Turn to page 85 for the answer.

PATRICK PICKLEBOTTOM EVERYDAY MYSTERIES

The Mountain Rescue

The school cafeteria was buzzing with energy as it usually was on Monday afternoons. Monday was pizza day, the one day each week that the cafeteria served something that the students actually enjoyed eating.

Patrick Picklebottom and his best friend, Claire, sat down in their usual spot along the far side of the cafeteria, and put their trays of food down. Claire began energetically shaking salt and pepper onto her pizza slices. "You really like your pizza like that?" Patrick asked her with a mixture of disgust and disbelief.

"Mmm hmmm," Claire mumbled, taking a big bite from the tip of her first slice. "It brings out the flavor in the cheese."

"Whatever you say," Patrick answered, taking a bite of his own, salt and pepper-less slice. He looked out the window next to him. Through the icy frost, he watched as a light snowfall dusted the ground on the playground outside. "I hope it snows a lot this week. My parents said that if it does, we can go skiing this weekend."

"Fun," Claire said absent-mindedly, more focused on getting the last few grains of pepper out of the now-empty pepper shaker.

Turning away from the snow, Patrick noticed a large crowd was gathered at one of the tables near the middle of the cafeteria. He nudged Claire, who was too focused on her food to notice much of anything else around her. "What do you think is going on over there?"

Claire looked up with mild interest. "No idea," she answered, wiping tomato sauce from her chin. "Maybe it's some movie star that heard about how good the pizza is here."

"I'm thinking it's not," Patrick said, and then, his curiosity getting the better of him, he put his food down and went over to see what the commotion was all about.

At the center table, Roger Wigglesworth was holding court. "I should have known," Patrick

At the center table, Roger Wigglesworth was holding court.
"I should have known" Patrick thought to himself.

thought to himself. Roger was a smug, obnoxious student in Patrick's grade, whose favorite hobby (other than picking on smaller kids) was bragging about himself, and telling wild stories about his heroics — most of which, Patrick suspected, weren't true.

Patrick asked Larry Angstapple, one of the kids next to him, what was going on. "Roger just started telling us about what he did over the weekend," Larry said in a hushed voice. "He said his brother almost went over the waterfalls in Bellbutter Mountains, but Roger was able to rescue him in time."

"Oh brother!" Patrick said loudly.

"Shhh!" Larry scolded. "I wanna hear this!"

Patrick mumbled, "Sorry," and turned to listen to Roger's story.

"So we got on our horses and our guide led us up into the mountains. Everything was going fine, when all of a sudden we heard a really loud 'Bang!' from out in the woods. I don't know what it was, but whatever it was, it really spooked my brother Mort's horse, because is reared up on its hind legs and galloped off into the forest! My parents aren't nearly as good at riding horses as I am, so I told the guide to take them back to the camp, and I took off after my brother. Silverback and I –"

"Who's Silverback?" Patrick asked.

Roger frowned, clearly not wanting to be interrupted. "Silverback was the name of the horse I was riding. I told everyone that when I started the story. If you can't keep up, you know, you can always go back to having peppery pizza with your girlfriend over there." The other kids laughed. Claire's crush on Patrick was hardly a secret.

"She's not my girlfriend," Patrick shot back, "but I got it — Silverback was the horse. Go on with your story."

Roger turned back to the crowd, "Anyway, Silverback and I rode for hours, but couldn't find my brother anywhere. As it got darker, I knew I needed to head back to camp, or I'd be stranded in the woods overnight. But I just had to rescue my little brother! So I kept riding on, and calling his name, but nothing.

"Once the sun went down, and it was too dark

to see very far, we had to stop for the night, and sleep in the woods. Seriously, I was pretty scared. The temperature dropped really low, and I thought for sure that I would freeze to death!"

Clearly unable to stop himself, Larry asked breathlessly, "That's crazy! Did you freeze to death?" he asked.

Roger blinked and looked at Larry through squinted eyes. "Hey genius — I'm sitting here, aren't I? Does it look like I froze to death?"

The rest of the kids laughed, and Larry looked down, "Oh yeah, good point," he said bashfully, his cheeks turning three shades of red.

Roger shook him off and continued, "So no, obviously I didn't freeze to death. When Silverback laid down to sleep, I remembered that horses stay warm in the cold temperature, so I laid down right up against her, and she kept me warm all night.

"The next morning, I was still very cold and hungry, but I couldn't think about any of that because I had to find my brother. Silverback and I continued riding and made our way down to a river, where I saw my brother's baseball hat near the edge of the water! I didn't know if it had floated there from further up the river, or if maybe he had stopped there to get a drink and it fell off, but then I saw hoof prints in the frost that must've been from his horse, leading downstream, so we followed those.

"I rode for a few hours, calling his name the whole time. I was starting to lose hope, and thinking that I might not be able to find him, when suddenly I heard his voice shout for help way off in the distance.

"It sounded like it was coming from the other side of the river, so I jumped off Silverback and ran into the water. I tried to swim to the other side, but the current was really strong and started pulling me along with it. That's when I saw my brother, holding onto a rock at the edge of a waterfall. It looked like I had gotten there just in time! But I didn't know how I was going to rescue him.

"I jumped into the freezing cold water, and tried to swim to him, but the current was too strong. So I grabbed onto a rock, too, but I was still too far from Mort. I looked around for a way to reach him, but the water was crashing into my face really hard, and I was having trouble breathing. I was afraid that I might fall over the waterfall myself, but just then I saw a really big tree branch come flying through the rapids towards me and heading toward the waterfall. I reached out and caught it just in time.

"Holding onto the rock with one hand, I was able to stretch out far enough with the tree branch to reach Mort, who grabbed the other side just as he was losing his grip on the rock, saving him at the last minute from being washed over the falls.

"Luckily, I'm a really good swimmer and I was able to drag the branch and my brother out of the river and back onto land. I was out of breath, soaking wet and freezing. We got back on our horses, and made it back to camp just before nightfall. Of course, my parents kept calling me a hero, but I don't think of myself as a hero — I just did what I needed to do."

Roger stopped talking and sat back, smiling, as the crowd of kids erupted in excitable conversation and congratulated him on his recent heroics.

Patrick spoke up over the crowd. "Hey Roger, I have a question for you."

"Oh yeah, what's that? You want to know how you can be as awesome as me? Well, let me fill you in — you can't!" Roger answered to the laughter of everyone else.

"No . . ." Patrick said, calmly. "I just wanted to know what you really did over the weekend, because none of this story actually happened."

How did Patrick know?

Hint: You may need to do some extra research to solve this one. What do you think you should look up?

Turn to page 87 for the answer.

The New Employee

Patrick Picklebottom put on his favorite green sweatshirt, brushed back his messy brown hair, and bounded down the stairs into the kitchen. Opening the refrigerator door, he grabbed a bottle of Fizzy's Lemonade, and snapped off a few squares of his favorite chocolate bar.

"Excuse me — put that chocolate down!" his mother scolded from the other side of the kitchen, where she was sitting at the breakfast table, reading a book. "It's eleven o'clock in the morning. You don't need chocolate this early."

"Patrick, listen to your mother," his father yelled from the adjoining dining room, which he had turned into a make-shift office for himself this particular morning. His red, pudgy face, usually always beaming with a jovial smile, was scrunched up in intense concentration. He sat at the head of the dining room table, surrounded by papers scattered in all directions. "And break me off a couple squares of that chocolate, while you're at it," he added, before turning back to his paperwork.

His mother rolled her eyes, sighed, and turned back to her book, as Patrick broke off more chocolate and joined his dad at the dining room table. "Whatcha working on, Pop?"

"I need to hire somebody down at the store," his dad said, taking the chocolate and putting a small square in his mouth, "so I'm looking through resumes and things to try and decide who to hire."

Patrick's father owned a gourmet supermarket in town, where Patrick often worked during breaks from schools and on some weekends. The store wasn't very large, but it seemed to have all of the products most of the people in town needed, so it was usually pretty crowded. Patrick especially liked the dessert corner, which was always stocked with his favorite treats.

"What position are you hiring for?" Patrick asked.

"I need a new night manager," his dad answered, not looking up from a sheet of paper in his hand. "You know Mr. Griffinbopper? He told me the other day that he wants to retire at the end of the month, so I need to find someone to replace him."

Mr. Griffinbopper was an elderly gentleman who helped manage the store every night and some weekends. Patrick liked working for him — he was always telling jokes and doing what he could to make working more fun. "Really? That's too bad — he's a great guy!"

"He is. He's going to be tough to replace," his dad mumbled, putting two more pieces of chocolate into his mouth. "He's worked for me for nearly ten years. I don't know how I'm going to find somebody who'll be able to run it as well as he does when I'm not there."

Patrick picked up a piece of paper from the table. The top of the paper had a name typed in bold letters:

DOUGLAS HOGGLESTOT

It was followed by a lot of very small type below it. "Is this one of the people you might hire?"

Patrick's father gave a quick glance at the sheet of paper that Patrick was holding. "That's called a résumé. It lists out a person's qualifications — you know, what they're good at, what their goals are, and it tells me about their past work experiences. From the look of his resume, Douglas might be the perfect fit."

Patrick read the sheet more closely. Douglas had graduated from a small community college about ten years earlier. Most of his career experience since then had been working in a variety of stores, first as a cashier or stock boy, and more recently on the management level.

But there was only one grocery store listed among his previous experience, and it was the last place he worked:

Night Manager, Pigsniffle's Market   **Bowlakes, Florida**

February – October

Pigsniffle's Market is one of the largest grocery stores in Bowlakes, Florida. As Night Manager, I was responsible for:

- Helping customers who shopped in the evening
- Making sure all shelves were stocked with food for the next morning
- Managing a staff of eight people
- Keeping customers happy and helping them find items that they needed

---

"It says his last job was as a night manager of a grocery store in Florida," Patrick said, "but the dates that he worked there were from February to October. That's less than a year. Didn't he like working at a grocery store?"

"Good observation, Patrick," his dad said, raising his eyebrows, and looking genuinely impressed. "I asked him about that when I interviewed him yesterday. He said he loved working there, but he wanted to move out of Florida because he doesn't like the heat and humidity."

Patrick's family lived just outside of Boston, Massachusetts, in a small town called Shufflebutter. While the winters were pretty cold, the summers were warm and comfortable. Patrick remembered going to Florida on a family vacation two summers earlier, and sweating so much he had to change his t-shirt twice before lunch, and he had barely even moved. "I don't blame him. Florida was nice, but it's too hot for me, too."

His dad laughed. "Yeah, it's not for everybody. But the point is, he didn't leave the job because he didn't like it or he wasn't good at it. In fact, I have a letter of recommendation from his previous employer here someplace."

"What's that?" Patrick asked.

"A letter of recommendation? It's basically just a

"What is a letter of recommendation?" Patrick asked,
as his dad sifted through his disorganized sheets of paper.

positive letter that someone writes about someone else. This one was written by his last boss, and lets me know that he would do a good job." His dad finally pulled a wrinkled page from underneath a bunch of other wrinkled pages. "Here, take a look."

Patrick took the letter and read it out loud:

November 12

Kenneth Picklebottom
Owner
Picklebottom's Gourmet Grocery
42 Strewsberry Road
Shufflebutter, MA

Dear Mr. Picklebottom,

Douglas Hogglestot was a wonderful employee who worked in our store for about nine months this past year.

Night after night, Douglas would come to work on time and ready. He is organized, hard-working and anxious to do a good job. He earned the respect of the people he managed, as well as his bosses.

He has proven to be a great team member, skilled worker and an individual that I admire. Based on my experience with Douglas, I fully recommend him for any job that he applies for and know he will be a great employee.

Respectfully,

Oliver Ogglestree

Oliver Ogglestree
General Manager
Pigsniffle's Market

"See?" his dad asked. "It's a really good recommendation from his old boss. I have a few other resumes to go through, but I think Douglas is my guy."

Patrick looked over the résumé, and read through the letter of recommendation again. "Does everybody always tell the truth on their résumé?" Patrick asked.

"Unfortunately, no. I mean, most people won't out-right lie about their skills or experiences, but they do tend to exaggerate their accomplishments when they put their resumes together. They're looking for a job, so obviously they want to appear as qualified as possible."

"And what about the letter of recommendation?" Patrick pressed his dad. "Would an employer ever write that a person was good at his job when he actually wasn't?"

Patrick's father considered this. "I don't think it's common, but yes, it does happen."

Mr. Picklebottom continued looking through different resumes on the table when he suddenly stopped. Looking up at Patrick quizzically, he asked, "Out of curiosity . . . why are you asking?"

"Because I don't think Douglas is the right person to hire. I think you need to keep looking."

Why did Patrick feel that Douglas was not the right man for the job?

Hint: No additional research is needed — all of the clues you need for this one are right in the story!

Turn to page 89 for the answer.

PATRICK PICKLEBOTTOM
EVERYDAY MYSTERIES

The Baking Contest

"**W**ow, what happened here?" Patrick Picklebottom stared at the wide, thin layer of white powder that covered the dark green floor and blocked the entrance to the food pantry in the school's home economics room.

"I accidentally dropped a bag of flour, and it got everywhere," Ravi Sniggleberry admitted, shaking his head and looking at the floor. "I was in a rush to finish the cake I was making for the baking contest, and, well . . . you know me."

Patrick conceded — he did indeed know Ravi. Jovial and friendly, with his shaggy blonde hair always in his eyes, Ravi was well liked, but known to be very clumsy. If there was a spill on the floor or a desk, chances were that Ravi was somewhere nearby.

"Are you sure it was only one bag?" Patrick asked incredulously. "It looks more like you spilled a whole flour delivery truck."

Just then, Claire Cobblepot, Patrick's best friend, skipped over to them, stopping short at the edge of the spill. "Wow! What happened here?" she asked, reciting Patrick's initial inquiry word-for-word.

"I spilled a bag of flour," Ravi repeated, and then, anticipating Claire's next question, added, "and yes, it was only one bag. I was rushing around trying to finish my cake for the baking contest later today. I went into the pantry to get the ingredients that I needed, and just ended up carrying too much at one time.

"Looking back at it, it was kind of funny. I was holding a big bag of flour, two bags of chocolate chips, a container of frosting, a stick of butter under my chin, and half a carton of eggs." Patrick and Claire laughed as Ravi started to mime himself holding too many ingredients at once. He wobbled around, pretending to hold invisible food, and continued, "I walked out of the pantry, and a box of graham crackers caught my eye. I turned to look at it, which made the butter start to fall out from under my chin. In a panic to catch the butter, I had to let go of either the eggs or the flour. I figured the eggs would be messier, so I let go of the flour instead. The bag split apart, and the flour went everywhere."

"Why didn't you just let the butter fall?" Patrick asked.

Ravi looked at the sea of flour that lay between them and the pantry door and considered this. "Now that you mention it," he said thoughtfully, "that probably would've been the best idea."

"So what did you do?" Claire asked. "Did you have to withdraw from the contest?"

"No," Ravi said, "I brought the rest of the ingredients that I had over to my workstation, then just went back into the pantry and got another bag of flour. And while I was there, I also took that box of graham crackers. You can never have too much of that!"

"That's very true," Claire said, squatting down next to the edge of the flour spill, and gently running her fingertip over it.

"What are you doing?" Patrick asked, his face

scrunched up in confusion.

"Just writing. It's fun — like taking the first step in new snow!" She continued moving her finger around the flour, until she finally stood up to admire her work. They all looked down at it, the smooth field of white now marred with the letters:

Patrick rolled his eyes. "Oh brother!" he said, sighing. And then, anxious to change the subject, he turned back to Ravi. "Did Mrs. Groomspittle get angry when you spilled the flour?"

Mrs. Groomspittle was the home economics teacher, and had a quick temper. A stickler for the rules, she wouldn't think twice about assigning extra work or even handing out detention for as little as speaking up in class without raising your hand.

"No, she wasn't here. Home-ec is my last class

Claire moved her finger around the flour. "It's fun," she said,
"like taking the first step in new snow!"

of the day, and I was really late for it today. I spilled a couple of cans of paint in art class, and had to stay after to clean it up. By the time I got here, everyone else was already done baking their cakes and was on their way out." Ravi looked at the clock on the wall at the front of the class. It was 5:02. "I took my cake out of the oven about an hour and a half ago and decorated it after it cooled, and the judging for the contest starts at six o'clock. So I still have time to clean up this mess before everyone comes back.

"What are you guys doing here, anyway? Did you bake something for the contest, too?"

"No," Patrick said, "we were just in the library studying for tomorrow's math test, and figured we'd take a break and come look at some of the cakes and stuff that are competing. So show us yours!"

"Sure!" Ravi said, enthusiastically. "Come on, I'll show you really quick, then I have to sweep this up."

They left the food pantry and walked to the front of the class, where a large assortment of colorful, delicious looking cakes stood in a row along a wide countertop. There were cakes of all shapes, flavors and sizes, from simple, vanilla-frosted bundt cakes to triple-decker, double-fudge layer cakes, and everything else in-between.

Ravi lead them to a short, flat, golden pound cake with chocolate icing near the middle of the counter. "There are chocolate chips inside, and the bottom is a graham cracker crust. I think it has a real shot of winning!"

"It looks great!" Claire said, her eyes wide and her stomach grumbling. "I wish I were one of the judges!"

"Thanks!" said Ravi, as Claire wandered off to look at the other contest entries. "Patrick, would you mind grabbing a dustpan, and helping me clean up the flour?"

As they began sweeping the floor in front of the food pantry, Patrick asked, "How did you bake the cake if you were the only one here? Isn't Mrs. Groomspittle's number one rule that nobody can use an oven if a teacher isn't in class?"

Ravi stopped for a second and hesitated before starting to sweep up again. "Yeah, I guess I sort of broke that rule. Do me a favor and don't tell anyone, okay? I don't want to be disqualified from the contest."

Patrick was quiet for a moment before he continued, "Don't worry — I won't say anything. But in fairness to everyone else who entered, you should really think about withdrawing your cake from the contest. We both know you didn't bake the cake that you showed us."

How could Patrick be so sure?

Hint: No additional research is needed — all of the clues you need for this one are right in the story!

Turn to page 92 for the answer.

PATRICK PICKLEBOTTOM
EVERYDAY MYSTERIES
The History Fair

It was April, and Patrick Picklebottom's school was hosting their annual history fair in their gymnasium. Kids from all grades were encouraged to enter whatever history-based project they liked. Some kids built models of the Egyptian pyramids or the Leaning Tower of Pisa; some painted pictures of famous people from history, like George Washington; and a few even put on funny little skits reenacting important historic events, like the first telephone call by Alexander Graham Bell.

Each student presenting at the fair had a square booth, with a table in front for small displays and a curtained wall behind it for hanging pictures and other items. As Patrick looked at his booth, he quite liked his contribution to this year's fair: hanging on the back wall was a very large, hand-drawn map of the world, with callouts for all of the largest and most important battles in World War II, the year in which each one was fought, who won, and how the outcome affected the rest of the war.

He was proudly showing his map to his best friend Claire, when he heard someone snicker behind him. Patrick turned to the front of the booth and saw Roger Wigglesworth looking at his map and laughing. Roger was a particularly obnoxious boy in Patrick's grade, who was best known for teasing littler kids, and bragging about himself, usually by telling stories that weren't remotely true. "Is that what you did for the history fair?" Roger asked in an insulting tone. "My cat could draw a better map than that."

Patrick and Claire looked at each other and rolled their eyes. Patrick was used to Roger and his insults. "Then your cat should enter something," Patrick said dryly. "He sounds very talented."

"More talented than you, that's for sure. If you want to see a *real* piece of history, come by my booth. Nobody else has anything like it at the whole fair," Roger said, as he walked away.

"Hmmm… What do you think it is?" Claire asked Patrick, as she watched Roger walk down the aisle towards his booth.

"I don't know, and I don't really care," Patrick replied, straightening out his map and frowning. "Do you think I should have used red markers here instead of purple ones?"

"Sure, purple would be great," Claire said, completely distracted. She was stretching her neck out as far as she could, trying to get a glimpse of what Roger had in his booth.

Patrick sighed heavily. "Do you want to go see what's so great about his presentation?"

"Well . . . okay, but only since you really want to!" Before Patrick could protest, Claire grabbed his wrist and pulled him briskly down the aisle.

On the other side of the history fair, Roger's booth was attracting a lot of attention. A swarm of kids and teachers were all gathered around it, although interestingly, the booth itself was pretty bare. The table in front was covered with a white tablecloth, and three glass display cases stood on top of it.

The display case on the left featured a bronze medal engraved with a tall, winged angel holding a sword and shield. The medal was attached to a rainbow colored ribbon, and it was laying against a square piece of blue velvet. On the far right was a photograph of a soldier sitting in a dirt field, holding a rifle and looking off in the distance, the crumbling wall of an old building behind him. The photograph looked old, and was yellowed around the edges.

In between the two displays, and clearly positioned as the main attraction, was a larger display showcasing a single sheet of paper.

"What's all this?" Patrick asked Roger, trying not to sound too interested.

"This," Roger said smugly, "is *true* American history. The soldier in the picture is my great grandfather, Charles Wigglesworth, who fought during World War I. The picture was taken in France.

"And that," he said, pointing to the case featuring the medal, "is the Victory Medal that he was awarded after the war was over."

In between the two displays, and clearly positioned as the main attraction, was a larger display showcasing a single sheet of paper.

"And what's with the paper in the middle?" Patrick asked, stepping closer to it.

"Read it for yourself — it's a genuine letter that he wrote to my great-grandmother while he was there, and it's been in our family ever since. It's a true part of history, and way better than any silly old map made with magic marker!"

"Wow," breathed Claire, looking at the letter through the glass. Then, turning to Patrick, she said in an almost whisper, "I never like to give Roger much credit, but you have to admit — this is pretty cool."

Patrick didn't answer her, as he stepped in front of the display case to get a closer look at the letter. The paper was considerably torn at the edges and very wrinkled and brown, especially around the creases in the paper, where it had been folded to fit into an envelope. The ink was faded, and smudged in some places, but he was able to make out what it said:

December 12, 1917

My Dearest Evelyn,

I hope this letter reaches you well. Thinking about you every day, and looking forward to seeing you again, are the only thoughts that are getting me through these grueling, terrible days on the battlefield.

Even now, as I hear bombs exploding all around me, and I see the devastation of war first-hand, it's hard to believe that all of this is real. How did I go from working in my father's shoe factory a mere three months ago, to suddenly fighting on the front lines in the middle of World War I? It's impossible to conceive, and yet I am proud to be fighting for my country, alongside my new brothers in war.

I pray daily that this will be over soon and I can come back home to you. And I hope beyond hope that when all this is finally over, the world will never have to suffer through another ordeal like this, ever again.

Yours always,

Charles

Claire sniffled, and Patrick looked at her and frowned. "Are you crying?" he asked.

Claire blinked hard and ran the back of her hand over one of her eyes. "It's just such a sweet letter. To think of him all the way in Europe fighting in a war, all the while wanting to be with his true love back home. It's so romantic! Who knows — maybe one day you'll write a letter like this to me, and our great-grandkids can display it at their own history fair."

"Our great-grandkids? Wait — what?" Patrick looked at Claire, shook his head and changed the topic back to Roger's display. "It's not romantic — it's fake," Patrick said. Then, turning to Roger, he added, "I think you have this in the wrong fair — you should present this in the Creative Writing fair next month, because this letter is pure fiction."

How did Patrick know?

Hint: No additional research is needed — all of the clues you need for this one are right in the story!

Turn to page 94 for the answer.

The Broken Trophy

"**S**o what should we do today?" Claire asked Patrick as they sat in his room. Claire was Patrick Picklebottom's best friend, and being the outdoorsy type, sitting in a bedroom on a bright sunny Saturday was the last thing she wanted to do.

"I'm not sure," Patrick mused, he eyebrows furrowed in determined thought. A few more seconds of silence passed between them before Patrick's eyes got really wide and his face brightened. "I got it!" he exclaimed. "Let's take our favorite books, head over the Snuffleberry Lake, and read near the water."

"Ugh, you and your books!" Claire sighed. "Okay, better idea: how 'bout we leave the books here, but go down to Snuffleberry Lake, and see which one of us can jump out farther on that old tire swing?"

Patrick knew that he wasn't going to win this argument, so he got his bathing suit on, grabbed a towel, and together the two friends headed down to the driveway where their bikes were waiting for them. They drove down the road and around the corner, then followed a short path in the woods to Claire's house, where Patrick waited by their bikes while Claire ran in to put her bathing suit.

A few minutes later, Claire came out wearing an blue swimsuit with orange stripes. Claire stood by her bike, put one hand on her hip, tilted her head with a slight smile and asked, "Do you like it?"

Patrick, who had been looking up and studying a particularly interesting cloud formation, looked dumbly at her. "Um . . . like *what*?"

The smile faded from Claire's face as she straightened up. "Never mind, Patrick. Let's just go to the lake."

The two put their helmets back on, drove down Maple Avenue, turned left onto Sullivan Way, cut through the school yard, and came to a road where a small yellow house with bright blue trim sat off to their left. It was the house where Roger Wigglesworth lived. Roger was a particularly obnoxious boy in their grade. When Roger wasn't making up stories or bragging about himself, he could usually be found making fun of some of the younger kids in school and just generally causing trouble.

Typically, Patrick and Claire would have picked up speed and tried to ride a bit faster to put as much distance as possible between them and Roger's house, as neither of them would want to run into Roger if they could avoid it. But instead, a big commotion outside of Roger's house made them come to a complete stop to check out what was going on.

Roger and his younger brother, Mort, were standing on their front lawn, talking to a couple of police officers. Mort was the star pitcher for the Pythons, one of the town's little league baseball teams, and only slightly less obnoxious than his older brother. A police car, its siren lights still flashing red and blue on the roof, was parked in the driveway, and a small crowd of neighbors were standing around, watching what was happening.

One of the kids in the crowd was Alice Plumtickle. Alice was in Mort's class, a grade below Patrick, and lived across the street. "What's going on?" Patrick asked Alice.

"I'm not really sure," Alice replied. "I think there was a break-in at Roger and Mort's house."

Patrick got off his bike and walked toward the front of the crowd to hear what Roger and the policeman were saying.

"Okay," one of the officers said, holding a pad of paper in one hand, and a pencil in the other, "let's start over. Tell me again what happened."

Mort excitedly began talking first, "I got up this morning around eight-thirty, got dressed and went downstairs to have breakfast. After breakfast, my parents drove me to baseball practice on their way to see my grandparents out in Snickerville.

"After practice was finished, which was about an hour ago, I walked home since my parents were still out. When I got here, I saw my MVP trophy from last baseball season on the front walkway, broken into two pieces." He held up both pieces of the broken trophy, and showed them to the officer. "It's completely ruined! Someone must have broken into the house and attacked my trophy! Someone who was jealous of it!"

"Let's not jump to conclusions. Where was the trophy before you went to baseball practice?" the policeman asked.

Mort pointed to a window on the second floor of the house, directly above a brick walkway that lead to the front door, alongside a long row of well-trimmed bushes that stood between it and the house. "It was in my room, where it always is."

The policeman pressed further. "And where in your room was the trophy?"

Mort hesitated, as though he didn't want to answer this question. "Well . . ." he said bashfully, "it was just inside of the window. I keep it there so I can show it off to the rest of the neighborhood. I especially want Alice Plumtickle to see it. I beat her out for MVP last season, and it got her really mad. I wouldn't be surprised if she were the one who broke in and destroyed my trophy!"

Alice stepped forward from the crowd to

"Someone must have broken into the house and attacked my trophy! Someone who was jealous of it!" Mort exclaimed.

protest. "Don't blame me! I was at baseball practice with you! You even got home before I did, because my dad and I stopped off for some ice cream afterward. The police were already here when I got home. You can ask my dad!"

The police looked up at Mr. Plumtickle, Alice's father, who was standing in the crowd behind her and nodding in agreement.

"Well, if it wasn't Alice," Mort quickly injected, "it must have been my brother, Roger. He's the only other one who was home at the time!"

The policeman turned to Roger. "Is that true? Were you home? Did you break Mort's trophy?"

The look of anger on Roger's face was unmistakable. "I already told Mort when he got home — I didn't go into his room, and I didn't touch his stupid trophy. I was down in the basement the whole time, doing homework. The dumb thing just fell out of the window by accident. Mort's just being dramatic."

"I am not!" Mort yelled back, clearly upset.

"Alright, alright, settle down. Do you boys mind if we go inside and take a look in Mort's room for any clues?"

"Knock yourself out," Roger said, still sneering at his brother. "The front door is open. Mort's room is upstairs. It's the first door on the right. But I'm telling you, you won't find anything, because *your trophy fell out by accident!*"

"We'll get to the bottom of it," the policeman with the notepad said. Then, turning to the other officer, he said, "Why don't you go in and see if there's anything out of place."

"The only thing out of place is Mort's underwear, which he's always leaving on the floor," said Roger with a smirk.

Mort was about to retaliate when a noise came from the second floor of Roger's house. The crowd looked up to see the policeman open up Mort's window from inside the house and stick his head out, looking down and examining the yard below.

The policeman on the lawn called up to him, "What do you think? Do you see anything?"

The officer yelled back, "Other than an unusually large amount of underwear all over the floor, not really. There are no signs of a break-in."

"See?" Roger said, angrily. "I told you! Your stupid trophy just fell. Next time, don't keep it next to the window, idiot!"

The policeman handed the trophy pieces back to Mort, who looked completely dispirited. "Sorry, son," he said. "Looks like it was just an accident. Like your brother here said, next time just be a little more careful about where you keep your things."

The crowd dispersed as the two officers walked back to their car. "Excuse me, officers?" Patrick said to them, timidly. "I hope you don't mind me butting in. The trophy didn't fall accidentally — it was thrown on purpose, but not during a break-in. Roger did it."

How was Patrick so sure?

Hint: No additional research is needed — all of the clues you need for this one are right in the story!

Turn to page 95 for the answer.

A Donut for Everyone

For the most part, Patrick Picklebottom loved his school's Ultimate Frisbee club. It was kind of like football, but they used a Frisbee instead and there wasn't any tackling. Each spring, the team met twice a week for an hour after school to practice, and then they would have games against other schools every Saturday morning.

What he didn't care for too much, however, was having to play on a team with Roger Wigglesworth. Roger was a particularly unlikable kid in Patrick's class, who was always showing off or giving himself endless compliments. As if that weren't bad enough, Roger also loved picking on smaller kids, trying to get away with some scam or another, and just being generally rude to everyone around him.

This particular Saturday they didn't have a game scheduled, so they just had a late practice and played a game of six-on-six amongst themselves. Wanda Figwiggle, who had accidentally broken her big toe a few days earlier, sat on the sidelines, keeping score and cheering the other kids on. Wanda was by far the best player on the team, and the main reason why they were undefeated so far this season. Patrick, on the other hand, was *not* the team's best player. He could run quickly enough, but his Frisbee catching skills were abominable, and his throwing was even worse.

None of that really mattered to Patrick, though, since he cared less about winning and more about running around and having fun.

The sun shone bright and strong and a light spring breeze came off a nearby lake, keeping the air around them cool. By the time the game was over (Patrick's side lost, largely due to his three dropped passes), all of the kids were sweaty and tired, but in great spirits from a fun day of playing.

Coach Cramdoodle gathered the team on the sidelines. "Great job, everyone!" he said jovially. "Nice hustle, all of you. Patrick, you have to keep working on your catching, and Leslie, I want to see you make some better passing decisions, but overall you all did a great job! We play like this next week, and we'll beat the Screaming Comets and make the playoffs for sure!"

The team cheered, and Coach Cramdoodle continued. "Before we wrap it up for the day, who wants to run down to Bagripple's Bakery and pick up some donuts for the team?"

Roger immediately jumped up. "I can do it," he said loudly. "I'm the fastest on the team, so I can get there and back in no time at all."

"Well, I'm not sure you're the fastest on the team," Coach Cramdoodle said, "but you're fast enough for this! Take this coupon and here's ten dollars to pay for the donuts."

Coach Cramdoodle reached into his wallet and pulled out two five dollar bills, and a coupon for the donuts:

BAGRIPPLE'S BAKERY

SATURDAY SPECIAL
BAKER'S DOZEN
ONLY $9.95

1276 DONFIGGLE ROAD, SHUFFLEBUTTER, MA

He gave them both to Roger, who put them in his pocket, turned, and ran off toward the bakery.

While he was gone, Wanda picked up a Frisbee. "Patrick!" she called. "I may not be able to run, but I can still throw. Let's practice your catching. Go long!"

Patrick ran out onto the field, looked over his shoulder and saw a perfectly thrown Frisbee flying toward him. As the disc floated softly down toward him, Patrick turned and reached up for it, only to watch it fly straight through his hands and land gently on the grass a few feet in front of him.

"Really, Patrick?" Wanda asked with a disbelieving tone. "That was the most perfect throw in the history of Ultimate Frisbee. How did you miss it?"

Patrick shrugged. "I don't know," he answered. "I just sort of have a knack for missing them!"

Wanda rolled her eyes. "Okay, let's try again. You'll figure it out, eventually."

Wanda threw the disc ten more times, with Patrick missing all but two of them. She was about to throw it again, when Roger showed up with a box of donuts from the bakery.

All of the kids, suddenly realizing how hungry they were, ran to the sideline. Coach Cramdoodle jogged over with a few jugs of apple juice. "Roger, can you please hand out the donuts. Everyone who wants a cup of juice, gather around over here."

As the kids lined up, Roger began handing out donuts to the kids, deliberately avoiding Patrick as he did so. As he reached in and took the last donut for himself, he turned the box upside down to show that it was empty. "Sorry, Patrick," he said, clearly not sorry at all. "There aren't enough donuts for everyone. So I thought it was only right that the worst player on team — that's you — doesn't get one."

"Hey!" Patrick protested. "That's not fair!"

"Yeah!" Wanda said, her mouth full of chocolate frosting and sprinkles, "Patrick tries really hard! And besides, everyone should get one, no matter how terrible of a player they are!"

"What can I tell you?" Roger asked, mockingly. "I would *love* for Patrick to have a donut, too." This was untrue — Roger didn't like Patrick, and Patrick was well aware of it. Time and again, when

"It's only right that the worst player on team — that's you — doesn't get one," Roger said as he handed out the donuts.

Roger told a lie or made a false claim, it was Patrick who called him out on it, nearly always embarrassing Roger in front of others. Roger knew he was no match for Patrick intellectually, so he often resorted to petty annoyances to try and get under his skin. "There just isn't enough for everyone. I went to the bakery like I promised, gave them the coupon and they gave me twelve donuts. It's not my fault that there are thirteen of us on the team, and only twelve donuts in a dozen."

"No," Patrick said, snatching a strawberry donut out of Roger's hand, "but it *is* your fault that you ate one on your way back from the bakery."

How did Patrick know?

Hint: You may need to do some extra research to solve this one.

What do you think you should look up?

Turn to page 97 for the answer.

The Shattered Window

The bell rang and all of the kids in school gathered up their books, got up from their desks, and rushed out into the hallways on the way to their next class.

Patrick Picklebottom and his best friend, Claire, made their way through the crowd, heading to the cafeteria for lunch.

"What did you bring for lunch today?" Claire asked.

"I think my mom made me a peanut butter and banana sandwich," Patrick answered. "It's not my favorite, but we were out of grape jelly, so it's better than nothing. What about you?"

"I didn't bring my lunch. I'm buying from the cafeteria. It's chicken fingers day!" Claire replied, smacking her lips together. "I love chicken fingers!"

"So do I," said Patrick, "but I'm not really sure what they serve in the cafeteria is actually chicken fingers. I wish you luck!"

"As long as it tastes good, it's good enough for me!"

Patrick laughed as they turned a corner down to the long front hallway that lead to the cafeteria. On their way there, they passed the school's reception area, and spotted their friend Tony Bambamellon sitting unhappily in a chair outside the principal's office. Tony was a quiet kid, friendly with his classmates but who mostly preferred to spend time by himself. And definitely not the kind of kid who was sent to the principal's office very often.

"What's going on there, do you think?" Patrick asked Claire.

"Huh. No idea. Maybe we should go have some lunch then come back and find out."

Patrick rolled his eyes at her. "Or maybe we can go find out now, and *then* go to lunch."

"I guess," Claire said grudgingly, and they opened the door to the reception area and walked over to where Tony was sitting. "Hey Tony. What's going on? What did you do to get sent to see Principal Spooklittle?"

Tony frowned at them. "Absolutely nothing!" he spat. "They think that I broke a window. But I keep telling them I didn't do it!"

"So why do they think you did?" Patrick asked.

"Because," Tony answered, fuming, "I was outside during gym class earlier this morning, and was just throwing the ball against the wall. There were windows there, of course, but I didn't throw the ball anywhere near them. I left when gym was over, and that was it. I didn't break anything! Someone else must have broken the window after that."

"I don't get it," Claire asked quizzically. "If you didn't do anything, why do they think you did?"

"Because," Tony answered, "Roger Wigglesworth told them it was me. He said that he was outside having lunch and he saw me throw the ball at the window on purpose and then run after it shattered. But it's a lie. I didn't break the window, and if I did, I would have stayed and taken responsibility for it!"

Patrick frowned. Anytime Roger was involved, he knew something shady was going on. Roger was a particularly obnoxious boy in his grade, who enjoyed picking on others, lying, telling tall tales about his supposed accomplishments, and just generally causing trouble. "Which window did Roger say you broke?"

"The music room window. You know, at the back of the school."

"Okay, don't worry. Claire and I will check it out and get to the bottom of this. I don't trust Roger any more than I trust Claire not to steal my cupcake when I'm not looking!"

Claire rolled her eyes. "Geesh! I steal *one* cupcake back in first grade, and you never let me forget it!" she moaned, before adding, "Wait — we're going to the back of the school? What about lunch?"

"Come on," Patrick implored as he pulled her out of the office, "this is more important. I just know that Roger is causing trouble, as usual!"

They walked through the hallway, past the library, down the stairs, down one more hallway, and cut through the gym to the back of the school. It didn't take them long to find the scene of crime, as two teachers were kneeling next to a window, and Roger Wigglesworth was standing next to

Roger Wigglesworth was standing next to the shattered window,
talking very animatedly about what he saw.

them, talking very animatedly. Patrick and Claire approached them.

". . . and I was right over there, having my lunch under that tree," Roger pointed to a large maple tree about 20 feet away, "minding my own business, when I looked up and saw Tony Bambamellon throwing his ball against the wall. I thought to myself that he shouldn't be doing that. It's not safe, you know? Kids these days!"

The two teachers, who were still crouched down, picking up pieces of glass from the dirt, glanced up at Roger, but otherwise didn't seem to be paying much attention to him. Their apparent disinterest didn't stop Roger from continuing to tell his story, however. "Anyway, I was just peeling my banana when I heard a loud crash! I looked up and wouldn't you know it, but Tony had thrown his ball through the window! He looked around, all guilty-like, to see if anyone had seen him, and then he ran as fast as he could. I guess he didn't see me. Good thing I was there, otherwise he'd have gotten away with it!"

One of the teachers, seeing that Patrick and Claire were there, held up a hand to stop them from coming any closer. "Stay there, kids. We don't want you getting cut with any of this glass."

Patrick looked up at the window and saw shards of glass still jutting out from the now-broken pane. He looked inside and saw the music room was dark. "Mr. Pearlkipple?" Patrick asked. "Do you know if there was a music class going on when the glass was broken?"

Mr. Pearlkipple, one of the teachers who was picking up the broken glass, answered Patrick without looking up at him. "No," he said, "Not today. Mrs. Scrubmutter, the music teacher, is out sick, so there haven't been any music classes going on. Why do you ask?"

Patrick answered with a smile, "Because if there was, they could have told you the truth — that Tony didn't break this window!"

How was Patrick so sure?

Hint: No additional research is needed — all of the clues you need for this one are right in the story!

Turn to page 98 for the answer.

The Acorn and the Oak

Patrick Picklebottom and his best friend, Claire, sat in the shade of an oak tree in the backyard of Lindsay Tugfiddle's house.

"I can't wait for Lindsay's pool to be open," Claire said, longingly eyeing the in-ground pool on the other side of the yard. "Just a few more weeks. Best. Summer. Ever!"

Just then, Lindsay opened the sliding glass door and walked outside carrying three bottles of Fizzy's Lemonade. "Here you go! Sorry, Patrick, I know you prefer iced tea, but this is all we have."

"That's okay," Patrick said, taking the bottle. "This is just as good. Thanks, Lindsay. Claire and I were just saying that we can't wait until your pool is open for the summer."

"I know. Me too!" Lindsay said, taking a seat in the shade next to them. "But you know what I'm *not* looking forward to even more? In another month, Alvin graduates high school, and he's going away to college. I'm really going to miss him."

Alvin was Lindsey's older brother. He was tall and lanky, with thick glasses and a crooked front tooth. Patrick never thought that Alvin was an overly nice or outgoing person. "Really?" Patrick asked. "I thought you two didn't get along."

"Well, we didn't used to," Claire admitted. "Up until about a year ago he was kind of a jerk to me. He used to tease me a lot and never wanted to do anything with me. Back then, I couldn't wait for him to go away to college!

"But he's changed a lot this year. Maybe because he knows he's about to move away. He's nicer now, and we get along much better. We spend more time doing stuff together."

Claire, Patrick and Lindsey spent the next hour talking about other plans they had for the summer. (Claire didn't seem to have much on her schedule other than spending time swimming in Lindsay's pool.) Eventually the sun got stuck behind some large clouds, and they decided to head inside.

Entering through the sliding glass door on the back porch, they went into the kitchen, where they each took another bottle of Fizzy's Lemonade, then made their way up to Lindsey's room.

Lindsey's room was a testament to nature and unlike any other bedroom Patrick had ever been in. Nearly every inch of it was filled with something that had to do with animals, the environment, or the outdoors. On her walls were posters of all sizes with photographs of polar bears, panda bears, sleeping lions, trees, canyons, flowers, bees, berries and bugs. Her collection of stuffed animals featured more species than a small zoo, and an inordinate number of cactus plants were strewn about in various places, making it difficult for Patrick to know where to sit.

The only part of the room that wasn't cluttered was a square white table under the window next to Lindsay's bed. On top of the table, pushed up against the wall, was a small, green plastic bucket with holes near the bottom, sitting on what looked to be a wet dinner plate. The bucket was filled with soil, and a single stem with three bright green leaves was growing from the center.

"Alvin and I planted that a few months ago," Lindsay said, noticing Patrick examining a leaf. "It's really starting to come in nicely!" Lindsay's

"Alvin and I planted that a few months ago," Lindsay said.

"It's really starting to come in nicely!"

face came to life — she relished any opportunity to talk about anything in nature. "I keep it here, next to the window, so it can get as much sun as possible until I plant it outside in the back."

"What kind of plant is it?" Claire asked, joining them at the table.

"It's the start of an oak tree!" Lindsay answered. "You know that tree that we were just sitting under before?" Patrick and Claire looked out the window into the backyard. The only thing back there, other than the deck, the pool and a fence surrounding the yard, was a lone oak tree in the far corner. The leaves were just starting to grow back after the mild winter they just had, and a tire swing was hanging from one of the higher branches. Lindsay didn't wait for them to answer. "It's like, a special family tree. My parents planted it a few years after Alvin was born, with just a single acorn. And now look how big it is!"

Lindsay admired the tree through the window, before continuing. "We all really love that tree. Did you ever notice that we've all carved our initials in it, on the other side? It's like part of the family. I know, we're weird. Some people have dogs or cats. We have an oak tree!

"Anyway, just before winter, Alvin collected a bunch of acorns that had fallen from it. Of course, not all of them were good for growing trees — Alvin knows all about it, and taught me. We threw away any of the acorns that were cracked or had holes in their shells because those wouldn't work. Then we took the ones that were left and put them in a bowl of water overnight. If any of the acorns floated, we threw them away because those wouldn't grow, either.

"Then we went out back to that bare patch of grass above the pool, and filled this bucket with soil from that area. That's where we're going to plant this, eventually. Alvin says it's important to use the same soil that the tree will end up in."

"It looks like it's growing really nicely!" Claire said enthusiastically. "How long did it take?"

"Actually, I was starting to think it wasn't working, like we had used a bad acorn, or something," Lindsay said, examining the underside of one of the leaves. "I give it plenty of water and sunlight, but for the first two months, nothing happened. Then about a month or so ago, I started to see the tiniest little stem sprouting up from the soil. And now look how big it's gotten!

"Alvin and I will replant it in the backyard in a few months before he leaves for college. I know it sounds silly, but I like that this new tree came from an acorn from that oak tree in the back. It makes it kind of special, you know? And I like that my brother and I are doing this together."

Patrick and Claire both smiled at her. "That's really cool," Patrick said.

"Thanks! Do you guys want another Fizzy's?"

"Not for me, thanks," Patrick said. "I have to head home. My dad will be making dinner soon."

"And I'm going to invite myself over to dinner at Patrick's. His dad is a way better cook than my mom is," said Claire, as they both started walking toward the door. "Thanks, Lindsay!"

Patrick and Claire made their way to Lindsay's driveway and picked up their bicycles. "That's pretty neat that Lindsay gets along with her brother now. I wish I got along better with mine. Carl's about to go to college, too, and he's still a jerk."

"Yeah, I guess," Patrick said halfheartedly.

"What's wrong with you?"

"I just don't like lying to my friends."

Claire stopped strapping on her helmet and looked at him. "Huh?" she asked. "What do you mean? When did you lie to her?"

"Well, maybe I didn't exactly lie, but I didn't tell her the truth about something. And neither did Alvin. She just seemed so excited about everything that I didn't have the heart to tell her: The acorn they planted didn't come from that oak tree in their backyard."

How could Patrick be so sure that Alvin was lying?

Hint: You may need to do some extra research to solve this one.

What do you think you should look up?

Turn to page 99 for the answer.

Solutions to
"Patrick Picklebottom's
Everyday Mysteries!"

Solution to:

The Brazilian Artifact

Patrick was pretty sure that with a little bit of research, he could poke any number of holes in Roger's story. But there was one big giveaway: Roger told Tommy that he was *the only one selected out of over a thousand entries, partially because I speak Spanish, so I could talk to the natives.*

Even though Brazil is in South America, native Brazilians speak *Portuguese*, not Spanish. In fact, Brazil is the largest Portuguese-speaking country in the world.

Faced with this information, Roger had no choice but to confess that he made the whole story up, and the vase was actually just a replica from a store called Bed, Bath and Brazilian. He'd bought it on sale for $4.99.

Solution to:

The Stolen Bicycle

The temperature that day was 97 degrees, and everyone was clearly feeling very hot.

Roger claimed that he came home right after the seventh inning, poured himself a glass of Fizzy's Lemonade, and came out to sit on the porch. He further said that he had locked himself out of the house right afterward.

But the game had ended over an hour earlier, and Roger still had ice cubes in his glass. Considering the extreme heat, the ice cubes would have melted long before Patrick, Claire and Alastair arrived.

This meant that Roger must have arrived home *very recently*, and not over an hour earlier, like he claimed to have.

While that didn't necessarily prove that Roger stole Alastair's bike, it did prove that Roger's alibi was false. When Patrick pointed this out, Roger stammered and eventually admitted that he took Alastair's bike. "I was going to give it back," he said. "I was just angry that you hit that home run off my brother, so I took your bike to get even with you."

Roger gave the bike back, and they went back to the ice cream parlor, where Alastair was so happy to have his bike back that he bought Patrick and Claire a round of strawberry milkshakes.

Solution to:

The Mountain Rescue

Roger said that when nightfall came, the temperature dropped and he was afraid he might freeze to death. To survive through the night, he slept laying against his horse, Silverback, after she laid down to sleep, because horses stay warm in cold temperatures.

Roger was right about horses staying warm in cold temperatures. But he was wrong about Silverback lying down to sleep: horses sleep standing up. Although horses might lay down for short periods of sleep, it's usually for less than an hour — not all night, as Roger had claimed, and definitely not long enough for Roger to have stayed warm until the morning.

When Patrick pointed this out, Roger had no choice but to admit that he made most of the story up. He and his family had gone to the Bellbutter Mountains and took a horseback ride, but he may have slightly exaggerated the rest of the story — basically admitting that he never had to rescue his brother at all!

The other kids, annoyed at having wasted half of their lunch period listening to a made-up story, abruptly turned and left Roger alone and embarrassed, and fuming at Patrick for pointing out his lie.

Unfortunately, it didn't work out too well for Patrick, either, who went back to his own lunch table to find that Claire had not only eaten all of her slices of pizza, but had devoured his as well! "Sorry!" she said through a rumbling burp. "I didn't think you still wanted it!"

Solution to:

The New Employee

Patrick took the letter of recommendation and laid it out flat in front of his dad. "Well, I don't think his last employer, Oliver Oggletree, really meant all of those nice things he said about Douglas. It might be a really, really crazy coincidence, but if you look at the first letter of each line, and read down," Patrick took a red marker and drew a circle around the letters, "It looks like he was trying to send you a secret message."

Patrick's dad put on his glasses and squinted to see the hidden message. He read aloud, "Do not hire." He shook his head and rubbed his eyes before reading it again to make sure it was real. "I can't believe it. I have to give this guy a call and find out what this is all about."

Mr. Picklebottom collected Douglas Hogglestot's paperwork, and without another word went into his den and shut the door behind him. Twenty minutes later, he came out and sat back down at the dining room table.

November 12

Kenneth Picklebottom
Owner
Picklebottom's Gourmet Grocery
42 Strewsberry Road
Shufflebutter, MA

Dear Mr. Picklebottom,

Douglas Hogglestot was a wonderful employee who worked in our store for about nine months this past year.

Night after night, Douglas would come to work on time and ready. He is organized, hard-working and anxious to do a good job. He earned the respect of the people he managed, as well as his bosses.

He has proven to be a great team member, skilled worker and an individual that I admire. Based on my experience with Douglas, I fully recommend him for any job that he applies for and know he will be a great employee.

Respectfully,

Oliver Ogglestree

Oliver Ogglestree
General Manager
Pigsniffle's Market

"Well," he said, his voice still in mild disbelief, "you were right, Patrick. It was a secret message that he left there on purpose. He said that Douglas is a nice enough guy, but that he wasn't a very good employee, showing up late, stocking the food on the wrong shelves, not being very helpful with customers. He said he was about to fire him when Douglas suddenly quit because he was moving out of Florida."

"So why did Mr. Oggletree write him such a great letter of recommendation?" Patrick asked.

"Douglas asked him to write it, and Mr. Oggletree didn't want to hurt his feelings. Fortunately for us, he was able to leave his secret message in it — and you were clever enough to spot it!"

In the end, Mr. Picklebottom didn't hire Douglas Hogglestot, but instead hired Miranda Cobbkibble, an energetic, hardworking employee who ended up being the perfect choice for the new night manager.

Solution to:

The Baking Contest

Patrick had noticed that the spilled flour was a "wide, thin layer of white powder covering the dark green floor" and blocking the entrance to the pantry. In explaining what happened, Ravi told them that after the bag of flour broke, he put the rest of the ingredients he was carrying at his workstation, then went back into the pantry to get another bag of flour.

But when Claire drew in the spilled flour, she described it as "like taking the first step in new snow" — because it was smooth and untouched. If Ravi had really gone back into the pantry, the flour (especially against a dark green floor) which blocked the entryway to the pantry, would have had Ravi's shoe prints in it, rather than being smooth and untouched.

"Well," Ravi said sheepishly, after Patrick explained himself, "the truth is I really wanted to bake a cake for the contest. But after dropping the flour, I got frazzled and didn't think I'd have enough time to make one, so I ran to the bakery downtown and bought a cake instead. Entering the contest is part of my grade, and I didn't want to fail.

"But you're right — it's not fair to everyone else. I'll tell Mrs. Groomspittle and withdraw from the contest."

As everyone arrived for the contest judging, Ravi pulled his teacher aside and explained what happened. Mrs. Groomspittle appreciated his honesty, and allowed him to bake another cake the next day that he could be graded on.

In the end, the real winner of the contest was Claire, who got to try a slice from over 14 different cakes!

Solution to:

The History Fair

Patrick noticed that in his letter, Charles mentioned that he was *fighting on the front lines in the middle of World War I.*

At the time, however, Charles would not have known that there would one day be a World War II — so he would never have called the war that he was in "World War I".

After Patrick pointed this out, Roger admitted that none of the items that he displayed were his, and that he had just bought them on the internet for the history fair. He grumbled something about getting scammed out of $80, as Mr. Whippleberry, the history teacher, forced Roger to shut down his booth, and immediately report to the principal's office.

Solution to:

The Broken Trophy

Mort pointed out that he kept the trophy *just inside* the window in his room on the second floor of the house, to show it off to the neighborhood — the same window that the trophy was thrown out of. He claimed that either somebody must have broken in and tossed it to the ground below, or Roger must have done it.

Roger insisted that the trophy must have just fallen out of the window by accident.

Roger knowingly lied when he said that the trophy fell out by itself. When the police officer went up to Mort's room, *the crowd looked up to see the policeman open up Mort's window and stick his head out . . .*

For the trophy to have just fallen out, as Roger claimed, the window would have been open, and it would stayed open afterward. But the officer had to open the window, which means it was shut.

The only way for that to happen would be if someone closed the window after throwing the trophy out of it. Since Roger acknowledged that he was the only one home at the time, it must have been him.

Faced with this logic, Roger admitted that he was jealous of Mort's trophy and broke it on purpose. The police left, but not without first severely reprimanding Roger, who promised to buy Mort a new trophy to replace the one he broke.

Solution to:

A Donut for Everyone

The coupon that the coach gave Roger was for a baker's dozen. Roger either didn't read the coupon, or didn't know that while a dozen donuts is 12, a *baker's dozen* is 13.

There were 13 kids on the team (they played a game of six on six, and Wanda sat out — that makes 13). This means that there was one donut for every player there. Since there were only 12 donuts when Roger got back to the field, Roger must have eaten one on his way.

After Patrick pointed this out, Roger grudgingly gave Patrick the strawberry donut he was about to eat. The coach was so mad that he benched Roger for the next game — and Patrick just so happened to score the winning points!

Solution to:

The Shattered Window

Tony was accused of breaking the window of the music room while tossing a ball against the wall when he was playing outside during gym class. And Roger claimed to have seen Tony break the window and then run away to avoid getting into trouble.

But as Patrick stood outside watching the teachers clean up the broken glass, it occurred to him that if Tony had thrown a ball through the window from outside the school, the broken glass would be *inside* the school, instead of outside of it.

Roger stammered to explain himself after Patrick told the teachers that the window was broken from the inside, and eventually he was forced to admit that he broke the window himself when he was playing inside the empty music room earlier. He then tried to blame Tony for it, so he wouldn't get in trouble.

Roger was forced to apologize to Tony, pay for the broken window, and got two weeks' worth of detention for lying!

Solution to:

The Acorn and the Oak

Lindsay said that her parents planted the oak tree a few years after her brother, Alvin, was born. Since it was the only tree back there, it couldn't possibly be confused with any other tree.

She also mentioned that Alvin was graduating from high school and going off to college soon. That would make Alvin about 17 or 18 years old.

Oak trees don't usually start growing acorns until they are at least 50 years old, so there's no way that the acorn that Lindsay and her brother planted came from the oak tree in their backyard. Trees that are in more open areas may grow acorns after just 20 years, but that would still make it impossible for the acorn to have come from that particular tree.

"Why didn't you tell her?" Claire asked him, after Patrick explained everything.

"I don't know," Patrick said, starting to push

his bike down the driveway. "She just seemed so happy that her brother was being nice to her, and that the acorn came from their family tree, I didn't want to upset her. It guess it can just be our secret.

"Well . . . ours and Alvin's."

Hey kids!

Do you want Mr. Jay to
read his stories to your school?

Ask your teacher or principal
to contact him at
jay@meetmrjay.com

About the Author
Mr. Jay

Author Mr. Jay (Jay Miletsky) spent years writing general business books that were boring to write, and probably even more boring to read.

Eventually he found his way to the far more exciting world of children's books, releasing the best-selling, modern day classic, *Ricky, the Rock that Couldn't Roll.*

He has since authored numerous children's titles, including *The Bear and the Fern, Patrick Picklebottom and the Penny Book* and *Tyrannosaurus Hex and the Unluckiest Day Ever.*

Jay lives in New Jersey with his wife, Amanda, and his two kids, Bria Paige and Oakland Jack.

Other Books
by Mr. Jay

Ricky, the Rock that Couldn't Roll

Tess, the Tin that Wanted to Rock

Do Pebbles Eat Chili?

Patrick Picklebottom and the Penny Book

Patrick Picklebottom and the Longest Wait

Patrick Picklebottom and the Magic Beans

Patrick Picklebottom Mysteries

The Bear and the Fern

Beware of the Nose-Biting Monster!

Tyrannosaurus Hex and the Unluckiest Day Ever

Have You Heard the News?

DEDICATED TO
THE TRUE DETECTIVES